To Fred

First published in 2017 by Child's Play (International) Ltd
Ashworth Road, Bridgemead, Swindon SN5 7YD, UK

Published in USA by Child's Play Inc
250 Minot Avenue, Auburn, Maine 04210

Distributed in Australia by Child's Play Australia Pty Ltd
Unit 10/20 Narabang Way, Belrose, Sydney, NSW 2085

ISBN 978-1-78628-002-2
CLP160817CPL10170022

Printed in Shenzhen, China

1 3 5 7 9 10 8 6 4 2

A catalogue record of this book
is available from the British Library

www.childs-play.com

The
BIG RED
ROCK

Jess Stockham

One day, Bif was so busy eating his breakfast...

chomp!
slurp!

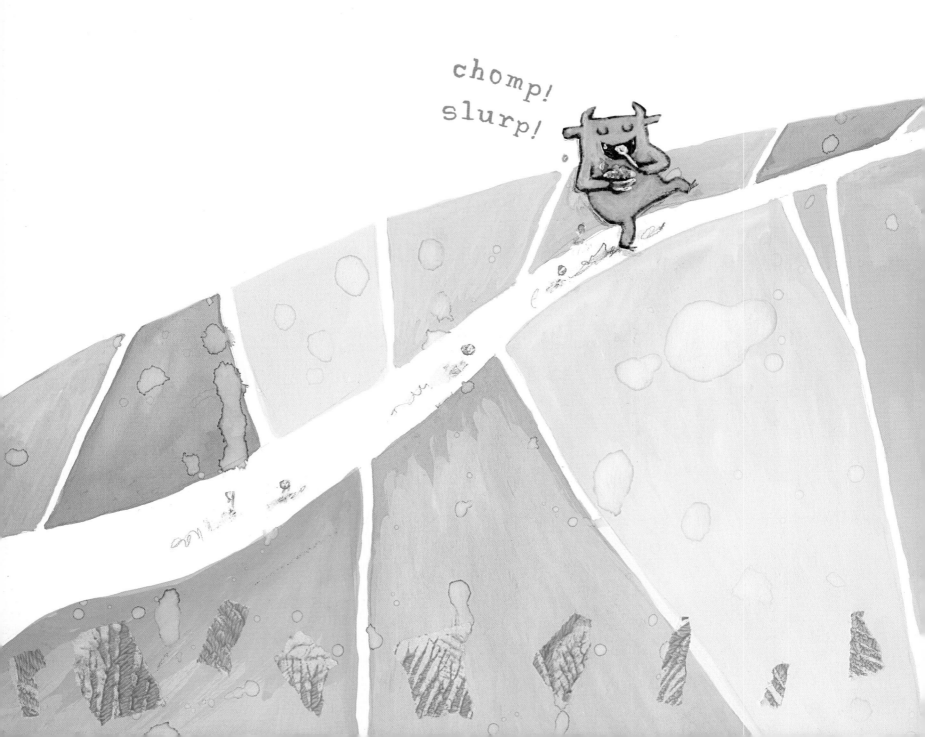

that he didn't notice
the Big Red Rock,

until...

Oi! Big Red Rock! You are in my way!

The Big Red Rock said nothing.

Then Bif remembered his manners,
and asked the rock nicely.

Get

"out of my way, please; please; pretty please; please!"

But the Big Red Rock didn't move.

So Bif tried
to kick it...

kick!

and bash it...

bash!

and push it...

push!
shove!

and pester it out of his way.

burn!

But the
Big Red Rock
stayed exactly
where it was.

Bif was wondering
what to do next
when Bop turned up.

Hi Bif!

Hi Bop!

"Can you move big red rocks?"
asked Bif. "This one is in my way."

"I can't," said Bop. "But I might know someone who can." And he ran off.

"Meet the Big Red Rock Eater!"
said Bop when he returned.
"She may be able to help!"

But the Big Red Rock Eater had a wobbly tooth.
She could only nibble small pieces!

So Bop ran off to find
someone else who could help.

"Meet the Small Blue
Rock Singer!" said Bop
when he came back.
"His voice is so loud
it can break rocks!"

But the Big Red Rock stayed in one piece.
So Bop ran off again to find some more help.

This time he returned with the Yellow Rock Crusher...

drill!

and the Green Rock Driller.

Then he fetched
the Orange Rock
Scarer...

scare!

quake!

the Pink
Rock Sucker...

Suck!

the Purple Rock Tickler...

tickle!

tickle!

...and a

Big Red Rocket!

Look out Big Red Rock!

But nothing could move
the Big Red Rock!

It was NEVER going to move... EVER!

"It's just a silly Big Red Rock that will NEVER, EVER move!" cried Bif. "Let's leave it alone and go and play!"

dance!

So they did...

until somehow...

on the other side of the Big Red Rock!

shake!

"That was fun!" said Bif.
"But now I'm starving!"
And he turned to get
his breakfast...

...only to find a Big Red Rock was in his way!